OH THOSE CRAZY DOGS!

A NEW FRIEND IN THE NEIGHBORHOOD! DIGGER!

BOOK FOUR

CAL

Illustrated by Rachael Plaquet

To order additional copies of this book, contact:
Xlibris
844-714-8691
www.Xlibris.com
Orders@Xlibris.com

ISBN: Softcover   978-1-6641-9554-7
         Hardcover   978-1-6641-9555-4
         EBook   978-1-6641-9553-0

Library of Congress Control Number: 2021921525

Print information available on the last page.

Rev. date: 10/20/2021

Oh Those Crazy Dogs!

Digger Takes Them on an Adventure!

This book is dedicated to Mark. For life experiences.

Introduction

This is a story about two crazy dogs, their adventures, and the mischief they get into.

They are very loving dogs, but they can't help getting into things.

Hi! I'm Colby! I'm big and red and furry! I love everyone, but sometimes people are afraid of me because I am so big!

Hi! I'm Teddi Bear! I'm big and white and very furry! I'm not as big as Colby, but just about. Everyone thinks I'm cute, and I put shows on for them.

Our owners picked us out specially and brought us home to love and care for us. We love them too, very much. They give us everything and a warm loving home. We will call them Mom and Pop

Sometimes we don't listen to them, especially me, Teddi Bear!

Our mom and pop love us anyway. Sometimes I get Colby in trouble. I can get him to do anything I want because he loves me too and can't say no. He protects me all the time.

DIGGER TAKES THEM ON AN ADVENTURE!

One day, Colby and Teddi Bear were lying down in the grass in the backyard. Both of them were comfortable but feeling a bit bored. Suddenly, they heard a kind of scraping noise. Scrape, scrape, scrape, scrape. "What is that?" Teddi Bear said to Colby. "What is making all that noise?" Colby slowly got up and walked toward the area where the noise was coming from. It was at the gate of the locked wood fence.

Scrape, scrape. Now they could see paws from another dog digging under the gate!

"Who is there?" asked Colby in a deep voice.

"Hi" said somebody in a high voice on the other side of the gate.

"Who are you?" asked Colby.

"Hi, I'm Digger! I live down the street. I thought I would dig you out of your yard and we could go play together!"

Colby and Teddi Bear looked at each other and laughed. "I'm Colby and he is Teddi Bear. One little problem though," said Colby.

"What's that?" asked Digger.

"We are a lot bigger than that hole. We won't get out with that one." Both Colby and Teddi Bear laughed. "Okay, boys, lets start digging!

They all dug at the hole on each side of the gate until there was a great big hole.

Colby said, "I'll go first. If I get stuck, you can push me, Teddi Bear, and Digger can pull me."

Colby went slowly into the hole and under the gate.

"Yay," said Digger, "you made it!"

"Yes, I did," said Colby.

"Okay, Teddi Bear, now it is your turn."

Teddi Bear peeked his head under the gate and said, "Are you sure this is okay? Mom and Pop won't like it if they find us gone."

"It will be okay. They're busy for now, we'll be back before they even discover us missing," replied Colby.

"Okay," said Teddi Bear.

Teddi Bear went through the hole and said, "Hi, Digger!"

And off they went, trotting down the street, tails high and wagging!

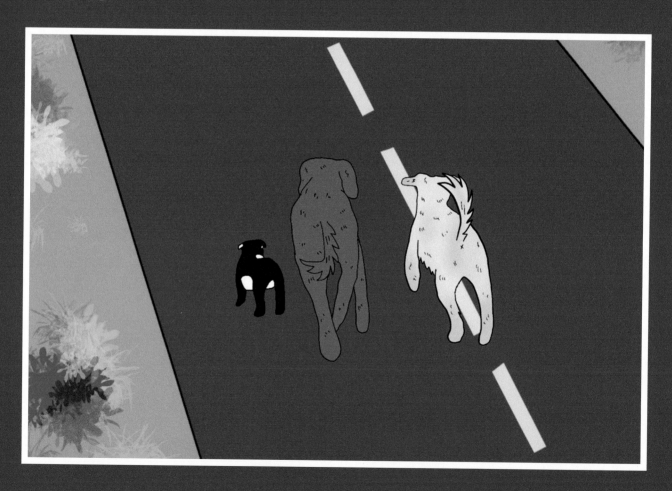

Colby asked Digger if he did this very often. Digger said yes, but he wanted to find friends to do it with so he wouldn't be so lonely.

Colby said, "Aww, that is so nice, happy to be with you."

"So," said Teddi Bear, "do you know where you're going?"

"I know everything around here," replied Digger. "What would you like to do?"

"Anything! We're free!" said Teddi Bear, jumping up and down.

Digger laughed and said, "Okay, but there is a very important rule or two. We must stay together, and we *must* make sure there are no cars coming in either direction before we cross the street, any street. If you forget and walk into the road, you could be killed. Please don't forget this, guys, it's your life I'm talking about. Okay, now where do you want to go?"

"Let's go where everyone goes to get food and all the things they buy," replied Colby.

"That's downtown," said Digger. "Okay, but it is a little bit of a way, so get your marching shoes on and let's go."

And away they went, tails high, marching together down the streets.

All three dogs were very careful crossing the streets, watching for cars.

"Wow, this is a real adventure!" exclaimed Teddi Bear. "I love this! There are so many new things and places and people. I just love it!"

"Me too," said Colby.

They kept walking past people until they got to the downtown district.

"Wow, is it busy and noisy here!" said Teddi Bear and Colby at the same time. "This is crazy! All the cars and people everywhere!"

Oh, the smells were incredible. They couldn't get their noses out of the air. The smell of food was everywhere.

"Wow," said Colby, "where do we go? What do we do?"

"Well, are you hungry?" asked Digger.

"Yes, yes," said Colby and Teddi Bear at the same time.

"Okay, so we go down these alleys behind the stores and restaurants, and we will find lots of food. Come with me."

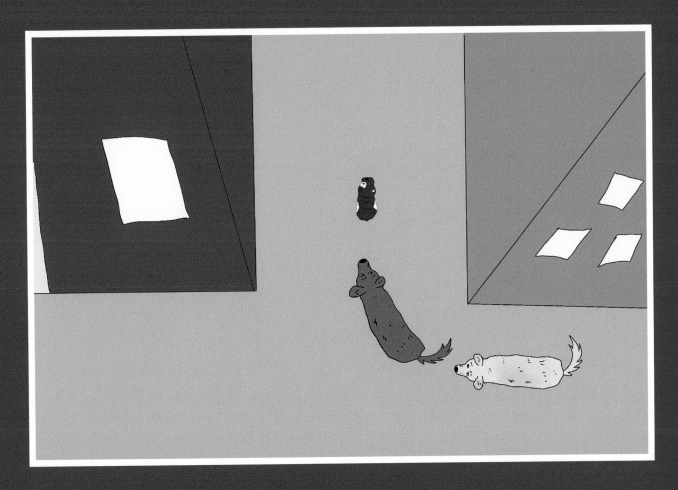

They all left the crowds and eagerly followed Digger into the back lanes. Teddi Bear and Colby just stopped.

"Oh my," said Colby. He had never seen anything like this! There was garbage and clothes and junk and everything you could think of, even people, in the lanes. Even food, and lots of it.

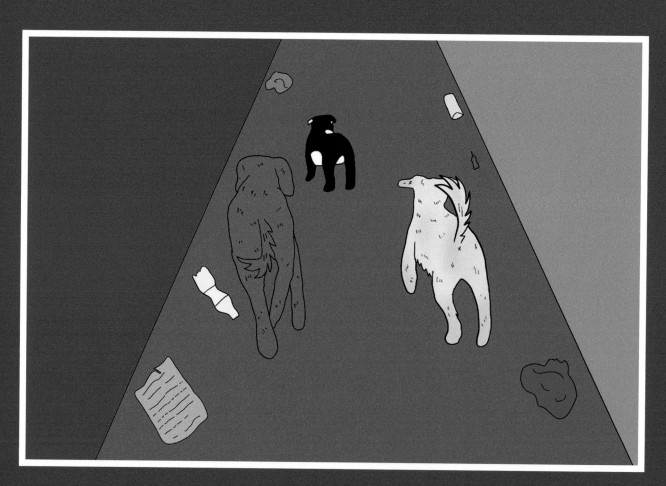

This was a very scary place.

"It's fine," said Digger. "Nothing will happen to you here! Whatever you want, take it, you can keep it and no one cares! It's okay, let's go!"

So Digger, Colby, and Teddi Bear walked down the long lane, checking out everything they passed. It was quite a chorus of sniffs. Sniff here, sniff, sniff there. Teddi Bear ended up with a straw hat stuck to his head. Digger had someone's boots on, and Colby had a dirty towel thrown over his back.

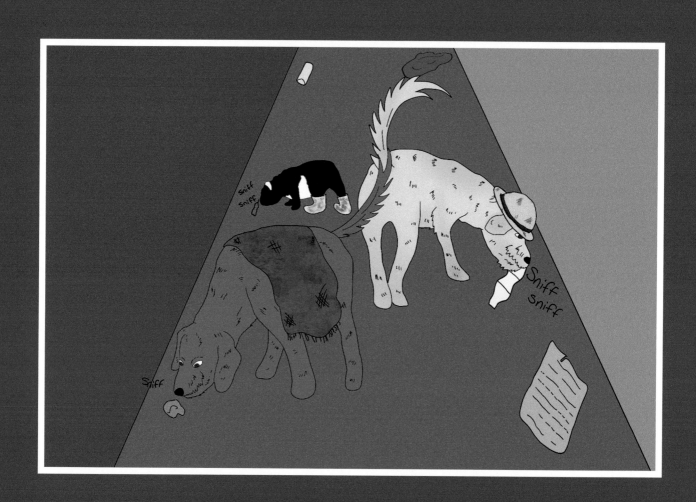

At every garbage can, the restaurants had thrown out uneaten food, and the three dogs had a smorgasbord of amazing food.

"What a waste!" said Colby. "We should come here every day!"

They were so full they could hardly move. And they were dirty! Oh my, they were dirty!

Colby looked around and realized he had no idea where he was. He asked Teddi Bear if he knew where he was, but Teddi Bear didn't. Colby said, "Digger, do you know where we are?"

Digger replied, "Sure I do. Why? Do you want to leave now?"

Colby and Teddi Bear both said at the same time, "Yes, we want to go home. I think our mom and pop are going to be very worried about us."

"It's okay," Digger said, "I can tell them what happened."

"Oh, like what?" asked Colby.

"Don't worry, I'll think of something," said Digger.

Colby looked at Digger and said, "I think the truth is what we will say. No point in making this worse. But let's try to get cleaned up first. We're pretty dirty."

"Okay," said Digger, "I see a couple of big puddles over there by the train tracks. Don't go near the tracks, just wash off in the puddles, and we'll go home."

The three dogs jumped into the puddles and started rolling around in them. The puddles were pretty deep. Teddi, who was a light cream color, came out of the puddle and shook the supposed water off. Teddi Bear was now black and slimy!

"Oh no!" said Teddi Bear. "What are we going to do?" Colby and Digger jumped out of the puddles too. They were also black and slimy.

"This isn't water! It's oil and gas from the trucks waiting to load up the train! What are we going to do?" said Colby.

"We have to go home and have a bath. This won't come out unless we have a good shampoo! Oh boy, Mom and Pop are going to be very mad at us!"

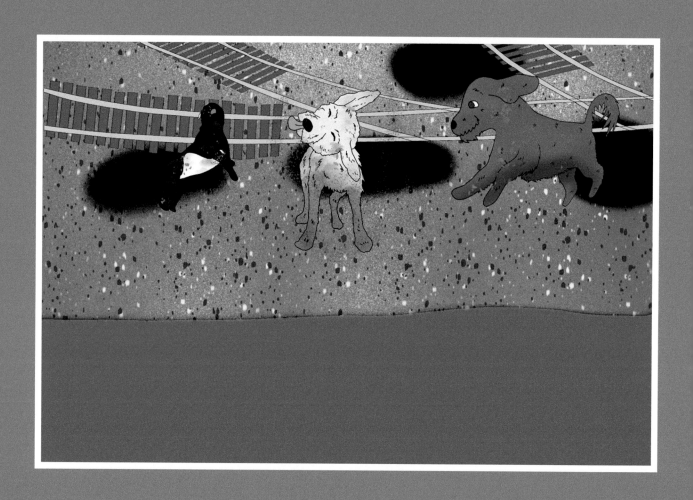

Meanwhile, Mom and Pop had discovered the dogs missing a long time ago and had been frantically searching for them all over the neighborhood, not suspecting they would go downtown. Not ever!

Digger led them to the backyard where they had dug the hole to get out. Colby and Teddi Bear squeezed back through the hole, getting even dirtier.

Colby turned and looked at Digger, who looked sad.

Colby said, "Thank you so much for this adventure, Digger, and we are so glad we met you. Please come again sometime, and we can do something else with you."

Digger smiled sadly. "Are you sure you want to see me again?"

"Of course, Digger! This was quite a new adventure for us, but now we need to go in and get cleaned up. You go home and get cleaned up too. We will see you later. Thank you!"

Colby and Teddi Bear looked at the pool longingly. "Nope, I don't think it is a good idea for us to clean up in the pool. I don't think that would make Mom and Pop happy. Let's wait at the door until they see us."

Colby and Teddi Bear waited at the door for a little while until Mom and Pop came home from searching for them. Mom yelled, "Oh there they are! I think it's them anyway. They are sooo dirty! Where have they been? What have they done?"

Mom said, "Let's get them into the bath right away. We can clean them up and get them warm and fed." Funny thing though, Colby and Teddi Bear were not hungry. "Oh dear, where do you think these dogs went?" asked Mom to Pop.

"I don't know," replied Pop, "but they sure looked ragged and dirty when they came back home."

Mom and Pop looked over at their two very oily, dirty dogs.

"I don't think we can wash them in the tub, we will have to bathe them out here on the driveway. We can't have that oil in the house. The dogs are far too dirty and oily to bring into the house."

"I'll have to fill in that hole and put a longer block along the gate," said Pop. "I think they had help digging that hole because it was dug from the other side too. We'll have to watch them more carefully because now they know they can dig out from under the fence. We'll find a way to make sure they can't get out again."

Mom and Pop looked over at their two very oily, dirty dogs. "We'll have to wash them again. The oil is still in their fur. We can't have that oil in the house."

So Colby and Teddi Bear were washed in the driveway over and over again until all the oil was out of their fur and skin. Then they had to put a conditioner on them because their skin was rubbed raw.

Mom and Pop towel dried them until they were reasonably dry so they could go into the house.

As soon as Colby and Teddi Bear got into the house, they were so happy to be clean and home they started running all over the house.

"Wow, what a fantastic day! I wonder if we will see Digger again? I hope so, he was fun!" said Teddi Bear.

It didn't take very long for the dogs to realize how tired they were after their adventure. They both went to their beds and settled down for a long nap.

Mom and Pop just looked at them and said, "Oh those crazy dogs!"

Thank you for reading this book, and we hope you look forward to our next book about Colby and Teddi Bear and their adventures in the swimming pool!

Oh Those Crazy Dogs! series written by CAL

Book 1: Colby Comes Home

Book 2: Teddi Bear Comes Home

Book 3: Teddi Bear's First Time at the Lake

Book 4: Digger Takes Colby and Teddi Bear on an Adventure

Book 5: Coming soon! Watch for it!